TIME-LIFE
Early Learning Program

Balderdash the Brilliant

Note to Parents

Balderdash the Brilliant is an interactive story designed to teach your child all about color. Throughout the book, holes in the pages highlight various colors and invite your child to guess what happens next.

Chapter 1, "How Color Came to Gray," challenges readers to imagine a world without color; it then introduces all seven colors of the rainbow. Chapter 2, "A Royal Mix-up," explains how primary colors are mixed to make the secondary and tertiary colors. Chapter 3, "The Quest," is a perceptual game in which a variety of colorful objects seem to change magically from one page to the next.

A handy reference guide to the colors of light and paint appears at the end of the book.

How Color Came to Gray

Between the White Mountains and the Black River lay
the kingdom of Gray, a remarkably colorless land.
Seasons came and went, but no one in Gray knew the
difference. Flowers bloomed and faded, but no one
noticed. From sunrise to sunset and from sunset to sunrise, Gray
was always the same.

During the day, the farmers harvested gray tomatoes, gray carrots, and gray corn. Their children colored their coloring books gray and flew gray kites across gray skies. At night, the people of Gray supped on gray bread and gray soup and went to bed. If they dreamed, they dreamed in gray.

It was all very dreary.

"It's all very dreary," complained the Queen. "What the kingdom needs is some brightening."

"Balderdash!" exclaimed the King.

"Balderdash?" inquired the Queen.

"Quite right," replied the King. "Balderdash the Wizard. That's who we need. I heard stories as a boy of his wonderful and magical powers."

"Then we must summon him immediately!" said the Queen, and she sent the Royal Messenger in search of Balderdash.

As the Royal Messenger hurried down the Gray Brick Road, he sang out to the Baker, "I'm off to see the Wizard!" The Baker told the Members of the Town Council, who told all their neighbors. Within an hour, everyone in Gray was talking about the Wizard.

"Balderdash the Amazing," said the Royal Zookeeper, "knows the language of all the animals."

"Balderdash the Wise can solve any riddle," added the Mathematician.

"Balderdash the Swift can fly from one end of the land to the other in a chair!" exclaimed the kingdom's Balloon Seller.

And so it went, with each citizen of Gray describing one wizardly feat after another.

In truth, the Wizard had not uttered a single spell nor opened his bag of tricks in more than 70 years.

"A summons?" he grumbled to the messenger. "I'm supposed to be retired. Whatever shall I do?" he asked his seven-year-old granddaughter.

Sage, a clever girl, replied, "We must leave for the castle at once. Shall we travel by chair?"

"Er, um…perhaps a walk would do us good," mumbled Balderdash, who had long ago forgotten how to fly a chair. "Um…find my bag of tricks, please. I can't recall where I left it."

As soon as Balderdash and Sage entered the castle's great gray gallery, the Queen addressed the Wizard.

"We'd like a bit of cheer here in Gray."

"Just so!" added the King. "Can you help us?"

Balderdash, who hadn't a clue how to begin, anxiously dusted off his ancient bag of tricks. The dust—all 70 years' worth—made him sneeze a colossal sneeze, and he dropped the bag. Out spilled a collection of powders, potions, and candles, along with a crystal that bounced across the floor.

Balderdash scooped up the crystal.

"I haven't seen *this* in a dragon's age!" he cried. "I've forgotten what it's for." He held it up to the window for a better look.

The crystal caught the light and split it into a dazzling array of color. "Zounds!" cried the Wizard.

"It's a rainbow!" exclaimed Sage. "I've read of such things!"

"*A rainbow,*" echoed Balderdash and the King and Queen.

Balderdash the Swift charged out of the castle, followed by Sage and the King and Queen. The crystal's rainbow spread across Gray's sky and bathed the land in RED!

The Fire Chief was jubilant! Never before had the kingdom of
Gray seen such a splendid fire brigade.

Then streaks and stripes of ORANGE!
The Royal Zookeeper was astonished!

The orangutan was overjoyed!
The oranges were delicious.

...liant blaze of YELLOW!
..." said the Farmer.
...s!" said the Farmer's Wife.
...ness!" said the Wizard. "What next?"

A fantastic flash of GREEN!
The kingdom's once-bedraggled dragon pre
Never before had the royal treasure sparkled

Then came a bedazzling burst of BLUE!
At the Gray Café, the Chef's blueberry pancakes sold
like hot cakes.

And the Members of the Town Council bought up the Shoemaker's entire stock of blue suede shoes.

A radiant rush of INDIGO!
A flock of indigo buntings perched on the clothesline.
And the clothes of Gray, once dull and drab, turned bright
and vivid and wonderfully gay.

Finally, a shimmering shower of VIOLET!
The violets were violet. And the King's robe turned a deep, rich hue.

"Royal purple!" exclaimed the Queen. "So splendid!"
"And so regal," agreed the King.
"I knew you would do something brilliant," said Sage.

"Not bad," said Balderdash, "for a retired Wizard."
The Members of the Town Council called it a red-letter,
blue-ribbon, rainbow-colored day. Everyone made merry.
And so it was that the kingdom of Gray was gray no longer.
"All's well that ends well," cried the Town Crier.
But as things turned out, he was wrong.

A Royal Mix-up

After the celebration, everyone returned to their colorful homes. At the castle, however, things were not so rosy.

"It's still gray," said the Queen. "But luckily there's someone here who can fix that."

"Goody!" said the Wizard. "Then Sage and I will be going."

"I think she means *you*, Grandfather," said Sage. "You have to cast a spell that will color the castle."

"Oh, all right," grumbled Balderdash. *"Razzle, dazzle, do!"* he cried hopefully. Two startled pigeons darted from the Wizard's pockets and landed on the King's crown, but the castle did not change color.

"No good, huh?" said Balderdash. "Well, then, perhaps this: *Ring-a-ding-dong!"* he urged, waving his arms wildly above his head. Three rabbits jumped from his floppy sleeves. The castle stayed gray.

"Okay, take this!" cried Balderdash, and he hollered out, *"Tap tappity bam bam!"*

"BAM! BAM!" echoed the door. Someone was knocking!

"Why, it's a delivery from the Quizzical Wizard Supply Company!" exclaimed Balderdash. "I wonder what I ordered *this* time!"

"Paint!" cried the Wizard in surprise. "Um, er—of course! That's just what we need to color the castle! But where should we begin?"

"How about in the Great Hall?" the King suggested. "It would look yummy if we painted it the color of this orange."

"Delicious!" said the Queen. "But we have only yellow, red, and blue paint."

"Hmm," mused Sage, "perhaps we could make some orange paint ourselves."

Just then they all heard two gushing, gargling waterfalls behind them. The delivery men had spilled the red and yellow paint!

"Ohhh, nooo!" groaned the grownups.

"Oh, yes!" cheered Sage. "Look! The red and yellow are running together to make orange!" She dipped her finger in the new color and held it up for all to see.

"My dear Sage," beamed Balderdash, "you're absolutely right!"

As the royal painters set to work coloring the Great Hall orange, the King pointed to his emerald ring. "Wouldn't it be fabulous," he asked the Queen, "if we could turn the Royal Game Room the color of this jewel?"

"Sounds lovely," replied the Queen, "but no green paint was delivered. Which colors can we mix to get some?"

"Well," said Balderdash, "if yellow mixed with red made orange, then maybe yellow mixed with blue will make green."

The royal painters swung into action. They poured two big cans of yellow and blue paint into a huge vat. To everyone's delight, the liquid turned green—exactly the color of the King's emerald ring! The painters used the new hue to turn the Royal Game Room gorgeously green.

"Balderdash, you're brilliant!" cried the King. "Why, I'll bet you could create a color for the Throne Room that matches my robe!"

"What a royal purple that would be!" said the Queen.

As Sage pondered the King's challenge, she recalled how they had made the other two colors. "We got orange by mixing red and yellow, and we got green by mixing yellow and blue. What two colors haven't we mixed yet?"

"Perhaps a spell would tell us," muttered Balderdash, leafing through his book of magic. "Let's see…should I look under 'R' for 'royal' or 'P' for 'purple'?"

Meanwhile, two painters had attached hoses to the cans and were spraying out jets of blue and red. As the colors flowed together, they produced a beautiful puddle of purple paint.

"Your Majesty, behold!" Sage called to the King. "We now have purple galore! It's a color fit for a King and Queen!"

this, the painters colored the statues of the
Sure enough, the purple paint fit the royal

looked on, she declared, "It's busy as a beehive
it reminds me—do you think we could make a
color of my hair?"

The royal painters rushed here and there, blend
and that: red with yellow, yellow with blue, blue wit
two colors would mix together to make brown.

Balderdash refused to give up. Finally finding a
in his book, he shrieked, "EUREKA!!!"

All over the Grand Study, startled painters fell o
dropped their brushes, and knocked over their buck

Paint was everywhere. Cascades of red, yellow, and blue paint swirled together, forming a lovely brown that was precisely the color of the Queen's hair!

"Maestro, you've done it again!" the Queen congratulated the astonished Balderdash.

"Perfect!" cried Sage. "Now we have seven different colors! I wonder how they would look on the outside of the castle?"

Taking Sage at her word, the royal painters splished and
splashed the seven bright colors all over the castle walls.

They rolled red and they brushed blue.

They spattered yellow and they speckled orange.

They flecked and freckled the walls with green, purple, and
brown paint until the once-gray Castle of Gray was a bedazzling,
seven-hued wonder.

"Hip hip hooray for Balderdash!" everyone cried.

A satisfied look spread across the old gentleman's face. "It's all in a day's wizardry," said Balderdash modestly.

"The castle *is* magnificent," agreed the King. "But why stop there? I wonder how many other colors we could make?"

"A splendiferous idea!" cried the Queen. "We'll throw a Color-Mixing Festival!"

The Color-Mixing Festival was held that very day. Citizens from all over Gray grabbed brushes and canvases and pots of paint and began mixing new colors:

The Fire Chief streaked orange through red and made a fiery vermilion.

The Royal Messenger mixed orange and yellow and proclaimed, "Marigold! I'll paint a field of flowers!"

The Chef whipped up chartreuse by blending green and yellow.

"Violet!" cried the Town Crier when he combined blue and purple. He trumpeted his discovery all over Gray.

The Shoemaker smeared green and bl... together. "Aquamarin... he exclaimed. "What beautiful boots I will cobble!"

The Royal Mathematician added purple to red and made magenta.

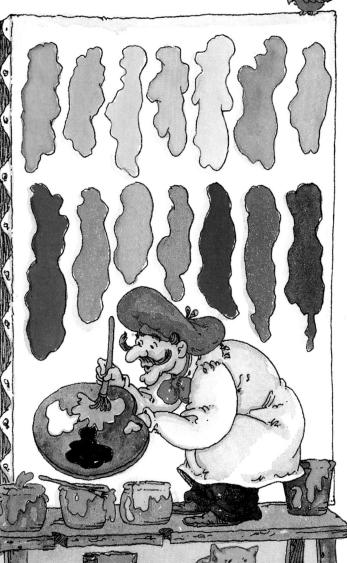

The Royal Artist mixed a dollop of white into each of his paints, inventing soft pastel colors. "Pink and peach!" he cried. "Chiffon yellow and sea green! Sky blue, lilac and tan! Just imagine all the paintings I can produce!"

Next the Artist added a smidgen of black to each color, creating deep and dusky shades: "Maroon and burnt orange!" he chuckled. "Goldenrod and forest green! I've even made midnight blue, plum, and mahogany! And look! Black mixed with white makes gray! Is there no end to the colors we can make?"

"There'd better be!" sputtered the Wizard. "These newfangled colors have got my head spinning round and round."

"Round and round," repeated Sage. "Grandfather, that's a wonderful way to remember all the colors! We'll put them in a color wheel!"

When the color wheel was constructed, the King and Queen placed the Wizard's crystal in the center.

The band, dressed in bright new uniforms, struck up a colorful tune: The trumpets blared red-hot jazz, while the bass thumped cool blues. Everyone danced and cheered, "Hooray for color!"

"Well," said Balderdash, "this must be my cue to say, 'And they all lived happily ever after!'"

Which just goes to show how difficult it is to see into the future—even when you're a wizard.

The Quest

The next morning, the Queen rose early to walk in the garden. "Our colors!" she shrieked. "They're fading!" Everyone came running lickety-split.

"My roses!" hollered the King. "Everything is changing back to gray!"

"And the crystal has been stolen!" cried Sage. "Someone with huge feet left us a mammoth note!"

"What gigantic nerve!" said Balderdash.

"We must get our crystal back," declared the Queen. "Follow those footsteps!"

Hey!
I took your crystal and a bunch of colorful things, and I hid them in the Land of the Giant. To get your crystal back, first find all the hidden objects. Then find me!
Yours truly,
The Giant

P.S. Have fun!

And so the Wizard, Sage, and the King and Queen set out on a quest to find the crystal and bring color back to Gray. They followed the footprints for three days and three nights until at last they reached the great wall surrounding the Giant's kingdom.

"Look!" exclaimed Sage. "It's the Giant!"

"Hmm," said Balderdash. "There's more to this than meets the eye."

"Maybe so," quavered the King, staring into what looked like the Giant's eye, "but I wish we'd sent the Royal Messenger instead."

"That's no Giant!" yelled the King. "It's a giant chartreuse frog!"

"GRIBBIT!" thundered the frog.

"The Giant left us another note," translated the Wizard, who knew the language of all the animals.

"Our clothes!" shouted Sage joyously. "They have color again! That means we're getting closer to the crystal."

"And closer to the Giant, too," the King worried. "Perhaps this is a job for the Town Council?"

"It's the Giant's boot!" interrupted the Queen. "The Giant must be very close by indeed."

"Over here!" called Sage. "Let's follow that nose!"
"Must we?" groaned the King. "It looks like the *Giant's* nose to me."

"That's no nose!" cried the Queen. "It's a jumbo pink flamingo!"

"Hop on my back," the flamingo sang out, "and I'll take you where you want to go."

"What sort of wild flamingo chase is this?" wondered the Wizard as they flew toward the Giant's castle.

"Whew!" thought the King. "It looks like the Giant is not home!"

"I'll give you back your crystal," the Giant continued, "just as soon as we've had some tea and cakes and a nice chat."

Which is exactly what they did.

In fact, they all had so much fun that the Giant joined the King, the Queen, the Wizard, and Sage on their journey back to the kingdom of Gray.

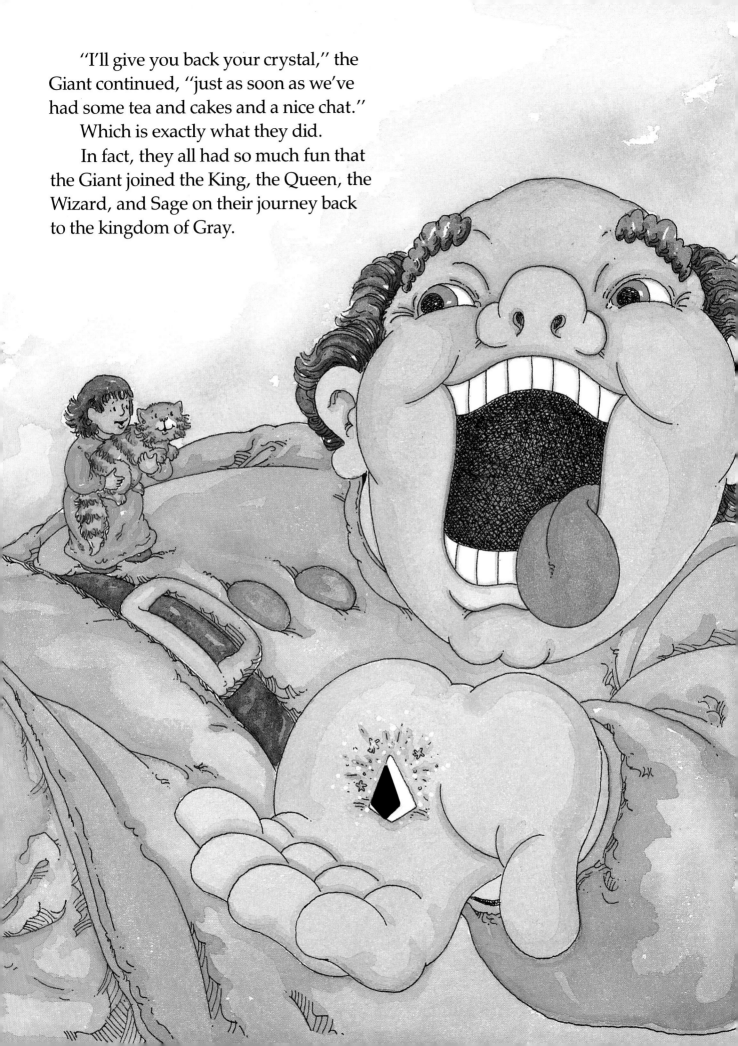

When the Giant carefully placed the crystal in the center of
the color wheel, all color was restored to the land of Gray.

The kingdom celebrated joyously; it may still be doing so today.

The King and Queen ruled wisely and well.

The Giant turned his land into a giant amusement park.
Children came from all over, and the Giant was never lonely again.

When Sage grew up, she set out to see the world. She returned
a year and a day later, declaring, "There's no place like Gray!"

And under the gentle spell of Balderdash the Wizard, everyone
in Gray lived happily—and colorfully—ever after.

THE
END?

The Colors of Light

What is a rainbow? The "white" light that comes from the Sun actually consists of seven different colors. Normally, these colors are invisible. But when sunlight hits the drops of water left in the sky after a rainstorm, it disperses—that is, it splits—into the seven colors, forming a rainbow. The colors of a rainbow are always in this order: red, orange, yellow, green, blue, indigo (dark blue), and violet.

Make your own rainbow! On a bright and sunny day, stand outside with the Sun behind you. Spray some water into the air from a garden hose or a spray bottle. (Be careful not to get others wet!) You should see a rainbow in the water spray.

How does a prism work? A prism is a crystal—a special piece of clear glass—similar to the one that Balderdash used to make a rainbow out of white light. Like water droplets in the sky, a prism splits white light into the seven colors of the rainbow.

The Colors of Paint

With just five colors—red, yellow, blue, black and white—you can make every other color! Red, yellow, and blue are "primary" colors. By mixing two primary colors, you can make one of the "secondary" colors: orange, green, or purple. The "tertiary" (third) colors are made by mixing a primary with a secondary color. Adding black to a color makes it darker; adding white makes it lighter.

Try mixing your own colors! A color wheel—a pie-shaped chart like the ones below—can serve as a handy guide.

A simple color wheel contains only the primary colors: red, yellow, and blue.

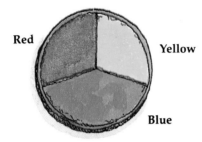

Red

Yellow

Blue

A slightly more complex color wheel shows the secondary colors (orange, green, and purple), which result when two primary colors mix together.

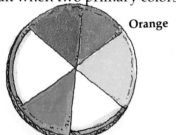

Orange

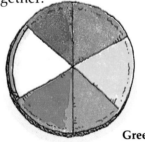

Green

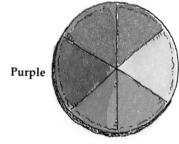

Purple

Orange is made by mixing red and yellow, so orange goes between red and yellow on the color wheel.

Yellow and blue mix to make green, so green is next to both blue and yellow.

You get purple by mixing red and blue; thus purple is wedged between red and blue on the wheel.

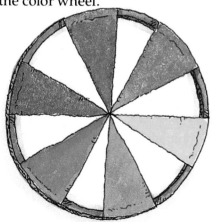

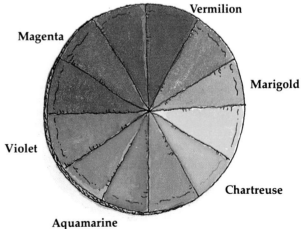

Vermilion

Magenta

Marigold

Violet

Chartreuse

Aquamarine

A complete color wheel includes the primary, secondary, and tertiary colors. The six tertiary colors are vermilion, marigold, chartreuse, aquamarine, violet, and magenta. Each is made by mixing a primary with a secondary color. Vermilion, for example, is made by mixing orange with red, so it goes between those two colors on the wheel. Try painting a color wheel of your own!

TIME-LIFE for CHILDREN™
Publisher: Robert H. Smith
Managing Editor: Neil Kagan
Editorial Directors: Jean Burke Crawford,
  Patricia Daniels, Allan Fallow, Karin Kinney
Editorial Coordinator: Elizabeth Ward
Product Managers: Cassandra Ford, Margaret Mooney
Assistant Product Manager: Shelley L. Schimkus
Production Manager: Prudence G. Harris
Administrative Assistant: Rebecca C. Christoffersen
Editorial Consultant: Sara Mark
Special Contributor: Jacqueline A. Ball

Produced by Joshua Morris Publishing, Inc.
Wilton, Connecticut 06897.
Series Director: Michael J. Morris
Creative Director: William N. Derraugh
Illustrator: John Wallner
Author: Muff Singer
Design Consultant: Michael Chesworth

CONSULTANTS
Dr. Lewis P. Lipsitt, an internationally recognized specialist on childhood development, was the 1990 recipient of the Nicholas Hobbs Award for science in the service of children. He serves as science director for the American Psychological Association and is a professor of psychology and medical science at Brown University, where he is director of the Child Study Center.

Dr. Judith A. Schickedanz, an authority on the education of preschool children, is an associate professor of early childhood education at the Boston University School of Education, where she also directs the Early Childhood Learning Laboratory. Her published work includes *More Than the ABC's: Early Stages of Reading and Writing Development* as well as several textbooks and many scholarly papers.

First printing. Printed in Colombia.
Published simultaneously in Canada.

Time Life Inc. is a wholly owned subsidiary of THE TIME INC. BOOK COMPANY.

TIME-LIFE is a trademark of Time Warner Inc. U.S.A.

Time Life Inc. offers a wide range of fine publications, including home video products. For subscription information, call 1-800-621-7026, or write TIME-LIFE for Children, P.O. Box C-32068, Richmond, Virginia 23261-2068.

Library of Congress Cataloging-in-Publication Data
Balderdash the Brilliant.
      p. cm.–(Time-Life early learning program)
    Summary: When a retired wizard is summoned to brighten up the dreary kingdom of Gray, he finds a very colorful solution.
    ISBN 0-8094-9266-0 (trade).—ISBN 0-8094-9267-9 (lib. bdg.)
    [1. Color—Fiction. 2. Wizards—Fiction.] I. Time-Life for Children (Firm) II. Series.
PZ7.B18126 1991
[E]—dc20   91-7129
                                                               CIP
                                                               AC